STAR WARS
THE LAST JEDI
™

ROSE TICO:
RESISTANCE
FIGHTER

JASON FRY

MY NAME IS ROSE TICO. A COUPLE OF MONTHS AGO YOU WOULDN'T HAVE RECOGNIZED ME . . . and I wouldn't have recognized myself either.

I was living on Hays Minor, a little frozen planet in the Otomok system, with my parents, Hue and Thanya, and my older sister Paige.

We had a quiet life on Hays Minor. Boring, even. I'd only seen other planets and star systems in holodramas—and dreams.

But Pae-Pae
(that's what I called
Paige) wanted to see
the ENTIRE GALAXY.

We used to make up
adventures where we were
in charge of traveling
circuses, or part of
a rescue team sent to save animals from volcanic
eruptions or supernovas.

Pae-Pae was always the leader, and I was always
her assistant. That meant I did all the dirty work,
but I didn't mind.

I loved my sister and wanted to be just like her;
SHE WAS MY HERO.

If you'd had the chance to meet Paige before she died, she would have been your hero, too.

PAIGE WAS CRAZY ABOUT FLYING. She would spend hours and hours using an old simulator that had belonged to our grandmother Etta, teaching herself to fly everything from old Z-95 starfighters to bulk freighters. When she turned 13, she began flight training with Central Ridge Mining, where our parents worked. Everybody could see right away that Pae-Pae was a natural. She could even make an old surplus OreDigger look graceful.

But while Pae-Pae was a natural, I was a natural disaster when it came to flying. I crashed every ship in the simulator. I'm still working on my piloting, and while I'll never be as good as my sister was, I know I'm getting better at it.

PAIGE MAY HAVE BEEN BETTER AT *FLYING* SHIPS, BUT I'M PRETTY GOOD AT *FIXING* SHIPS. I'VE JUST ALWAYS UNDERSTOOD MACHINES. IF YOU OPEN A MAINTENANCE HATCH AND LET ME POKE AROUND INSIDE, I'LL CRAWL OUT AND TELL YOU HOW IT WORKS, OR WHY IT'S STOPPED WORKING.

Paige didn't understand that stuff. She'd yawn when I tried to explain something, like how a rudder responds to a pilot's commands. Once, after a long day of training, she joked that I knew everything about our Resistance bomber except how to fly it. That made me so mad, and I yelled back that the only thing she knew about our Resistance bomber was how to fly it. When we stopped yelling at each other, we couldn't help but laugh, because we'd both been right.

As kids, Paige and I used to promise each other that one day we'd visit other planets—planets totally different from our own. Like planets with air!

Hays Minor barely even had an *atmosphere.* If you went outside without protection, you'd die in less than a minute! So we'd daydream about walking outside on a planet with rivers and grasslands and jungles, full of animals and plants. Eventually we got to do that, though not in the way we'd hoped.

Our grandparents settled on Hays Minor because they were prospectors, searching for a rare type of pure gold known as Haysian smelt. When they found it, they celebrated by casting two medallions shaped like the symbol of the Otomok system.

Paige and I each wore one of the medallions on a cord. The two pieces had fit together perfectly. Just like us. I miss her so much.

My medallion—the one that's left—reminds me of my home. The home the First Order took away.

They came to Otomok to recruit geologists and scientists, and made these big speeches about a better life beyond the galactic frontier. We just laughed at them— they were crazy and angry, and we thought their speeches were just big talk. We figured they'd never bother with a rock like Hays Minor.

BUT BY THE TIME WE TOOK THEM SERIOUSLY, IT WAS TOO LATE.

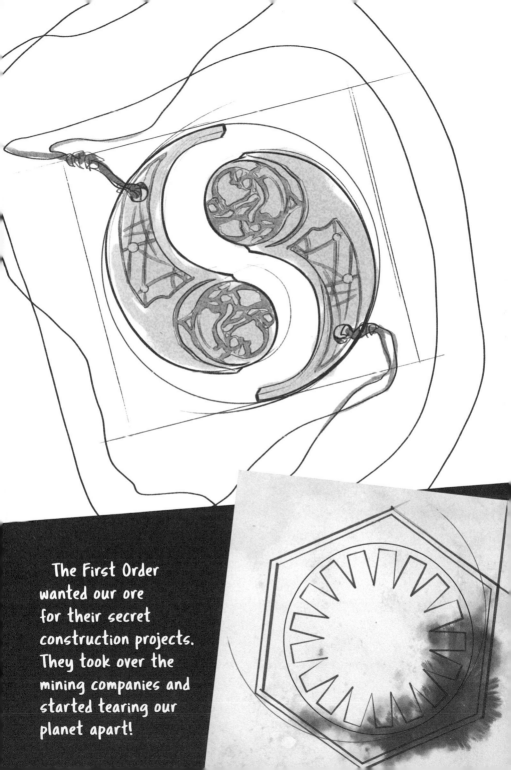

The First Order wanted our ore for their secret construction projects. They took over the mining companies and started tearing our planet apart!

That was when people started whispering about fighting back. Paige and I wanted to join them, but our parents ordered us to keep quiet. They understood what was happening to Hays Minor, and said it was happening on other planets, too. And they promised that they planned to fight back. But talking about it was DANGEROUS, so they urged us to be patient.

We tried, but then the First Order starting testing weapons on our planet, and invited arms dealers from all over the galaxy to watch. You'd see them in the spaceports and supply depots, wearing shimmering fabrics and lush furs that made us feel ashamed of our stained jumpsuits and patched cloaks. One day I touched the fur collar of a man's jacket. I just wanted to know what real fur felt like, but a second later a security droid had a magnetic grip on my wrist and a First Order officer was threatening to arrest me!

I HATED THOSE ARMS DEALERS THE MOMENT I SAW THEM. I STILL DO. IF GENERAL ORGANA WOULD LEND ME AN X-WING, I'D BLAST EVERY ONE IN THE OUTER RIM AND THE GALAXY WOULD BE A BETTER PLACE.

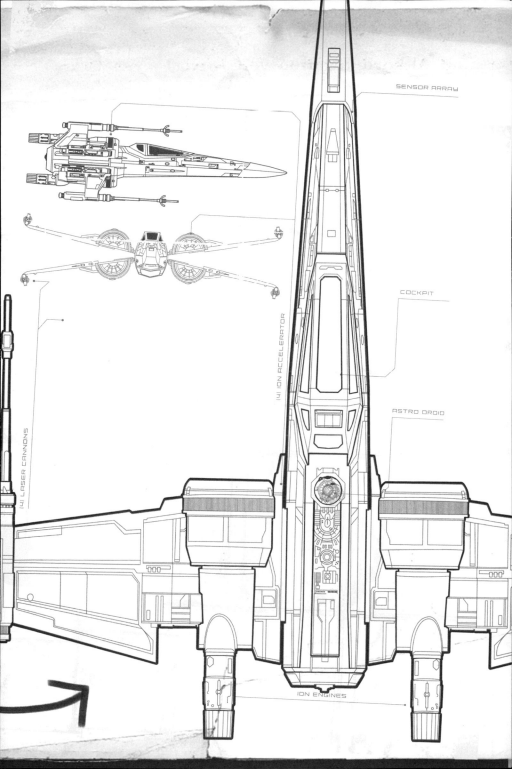

SENSOR ARRAY

COCKPIT

ASTRO DROID

(4) ION ACCELERATOR

(4) LASER CANNONS

ION ENGINES

Within a few months of the First Order's arrival, the pollution on Hays Minor was so bad that you could no longer see the stars. Pae-Pae and I asked our parents if now was the time to fight back, and they said it was.

But they wouldn't let us fight on Hays Minor.

Instead, they wanted us to join the Resistance. Mama and Papa said the galaxy needed to know what had happened, and thought that if two children of Otomok joined the larger struggle against the First Order, the Resistance leadership might find a way to fight for our star system. We didn't like the idea of being separated from them, but they insisted it was for the best, and reminded us that the two of us would still be together. SO WE AGREED.

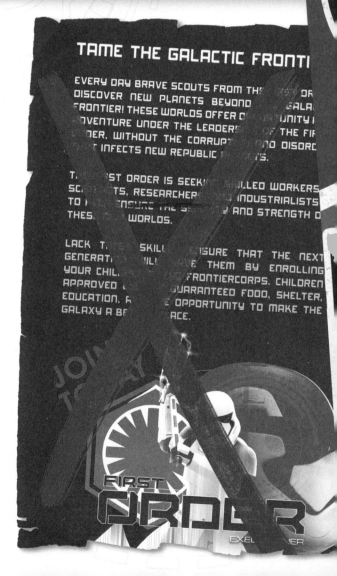

TAME THE GALACTIC FRONTI

EVERY DAY BRAVE SCOUTS FROM THE   OR
DISCOVER NEW PLANETS BEYOND   GALA
FRONTIER! THESE WORLDS OFFER C   UNITY I
DVENTURE UNDER THE LEADERS   F THE FIF
    ER, WITHOUT THE CORRUPT   O DISORC
    T INFECTS NEW REPUBLIC   'S.

T.   ST ORDER IS SEEKI   LLED WORKERS
SC   TS, RESEARCHER   INDUSTRIALISTS
TO   AND STRENGTH O
THES.   WORLDS.

LACK T.   SKILL   SURE THAT THE NEXT
GENERATI   ILL   E THEM BY ENROLLING
YOUR CHIL   FRONTIERCORPS. CHILDREN
APPROVED   UARANTEED FOOD, SHELTER,
EDUCATION,   OPPORTUNITY TO MAKE THE
GALAXY A B   ACE.

FIRST ORDER

EXEL   ER

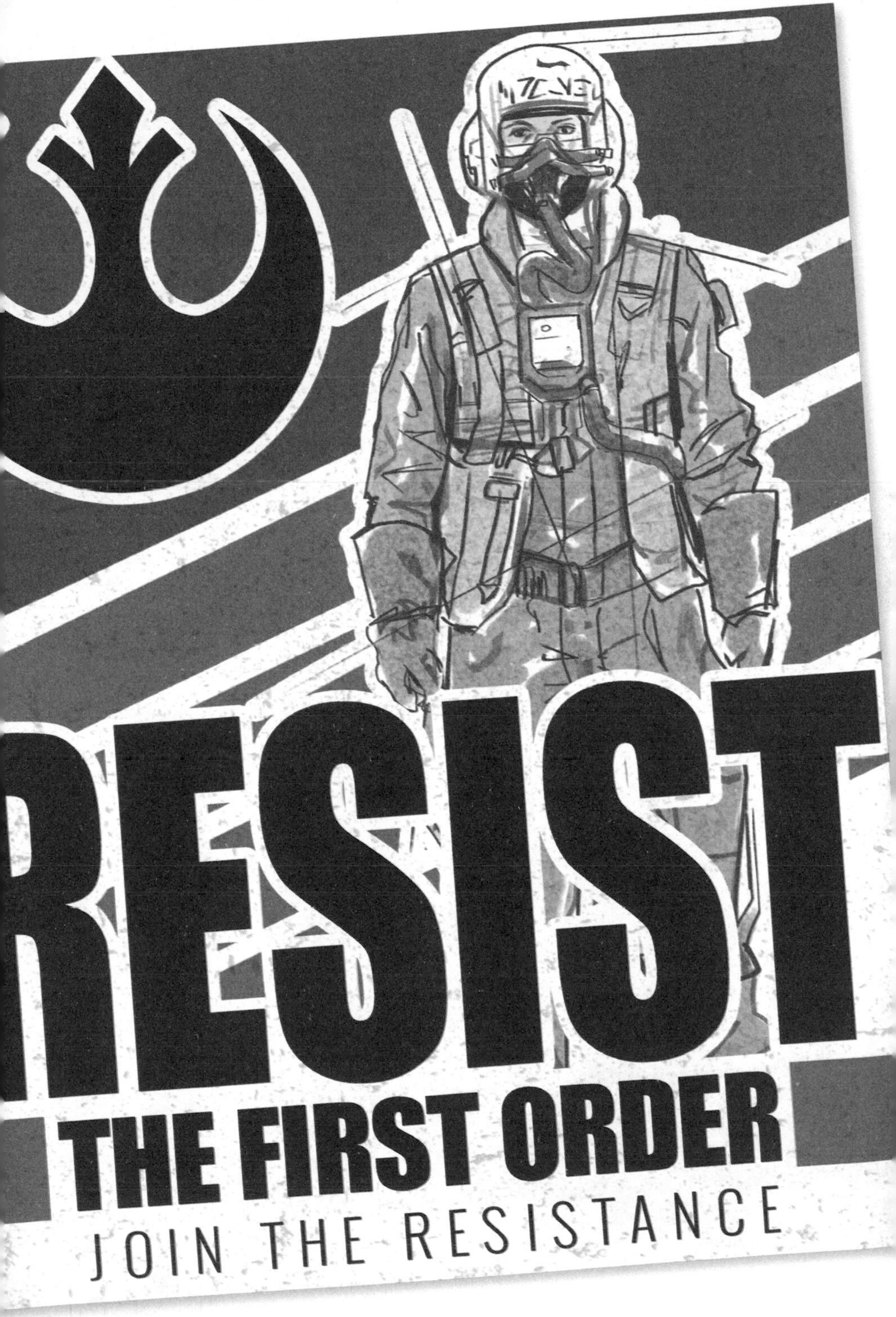
RESIST
THE FIRST ORDER
JOIN THE RESISTANCE

Our parents arranged passage for us on a supply ship to Botajef, a city-planet with so many ships coming and going that I couldn't count them all. There, we met a Resistance agent that Mama and Papa knew. She had us board a freighter, which brought us to the Resistance base on D'Qar.

I had trouble believing D'Qar was real. You could go outside and breathe without a mask! And the jungles! We'd never seen a real live animal, and now the air was full of birds and insects making this crazy, lovely racket. After every mission for the Resistance, Pae-Pae would sit in the jungle and watch little funny-colored lizards run up and down tree trunks, or try to coax a sonar swallow down from the sky.

Paige had hours and hours of experience aboard OreDiggers, which were just StarFortress bombers converted for civilian use. The Resistance made her a ball-turret gunner and promised she could work her way up to pilot. But they didn't know what to do with me. They wanted to hand me a hydrospanner and have me fix droids, but Pae-Pae told the bomber squadron's commanding officer, Fossil, that she wouldn't fly without me.

Fossil didn't like that, and she didn't believe Pae-Pae when she said I had the skills to be a flight engineer. Fossil made me crawl from one end of a bomber to the other, identifying every part, from the active trackers to the ion thrusters, and telling her what might go wrong with each one and how to fix it.

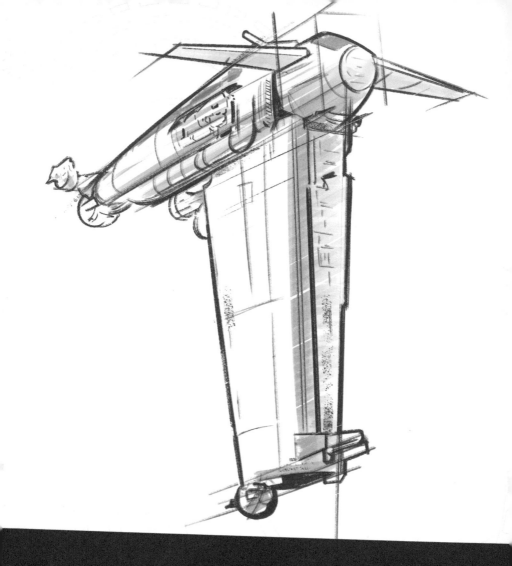

BUT I CONVINCED HER. AND SO PAIGE AND I JOINED THE CREW OF *COBALT HAMMER* AS SISTERS.

I thought we'd get to lead a bomber squadron back to Hays Minor, but that wasn't possible. The Resistance couldn't fight the First Order openly, because the New Republic still thought that peace with the First Order was possible. We all knew that wasn't the case, though.

We'd only been with the Resistance a few days when Fossil told us our parents were missing in action and the First Order had blockaded our system and intended to blow apart Hays Minor for ore! I wanted to go back, to do something to help, but Paige just pulled me into a hug and we cried. We knew we couldn't save our parents, or our planet. All we could do was keep fighting with the Resistance to stop the First Order from destroying other worlds and families like they had ruined ours.

And so that's what we did, *together.* We flew several missions, and I took on a project for General Organa to try and make our bombers hard for enemy sensors to detect. I dreamed up this crazy device I called a baffler, which combined engine baffles, emergency shunts, and fuel tanks. My bafflers looked weird, but they kept our bombers undetected during spy missions to the Atterra system.

But that project also led to Paige and I being separated.

ꜱ꜠꜡ꜰꜰ꜡ꜱ ꜰꜰꜱ

RADDUS MC85 STAR CRUISER

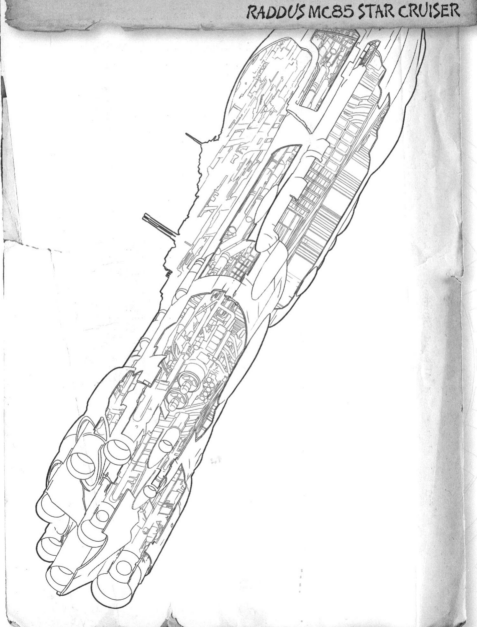

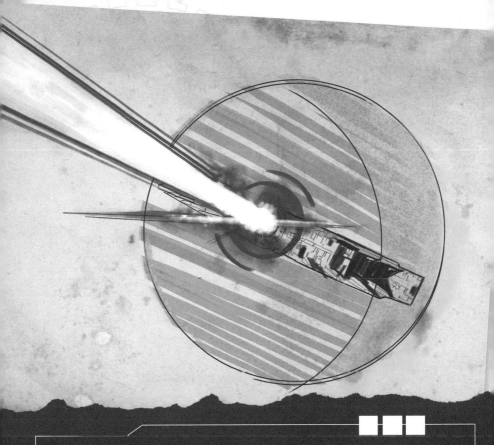

After our last mission to Atterra, Vice Admiral Holdo of the *Ninka* told us some terrible news: the First Order had destroyed the New Republic capital of Hosnian Prime with a weapon that could fire through hyperspace! The Resistance had traced the attack back to a planet that the First Order had turned into a superweapon called Starkiller Base. The Resistance had managed to destroy the Starkiller, thanks to a group of heroes who actually infiltrated the planet to lower the base's shields, and a brave team of X-wing pilots who fired blast after blast til the whole planet imploded!

But the First Order had tracked the Resistance back to D'Qar, and we had to hurry to evacuate our base!

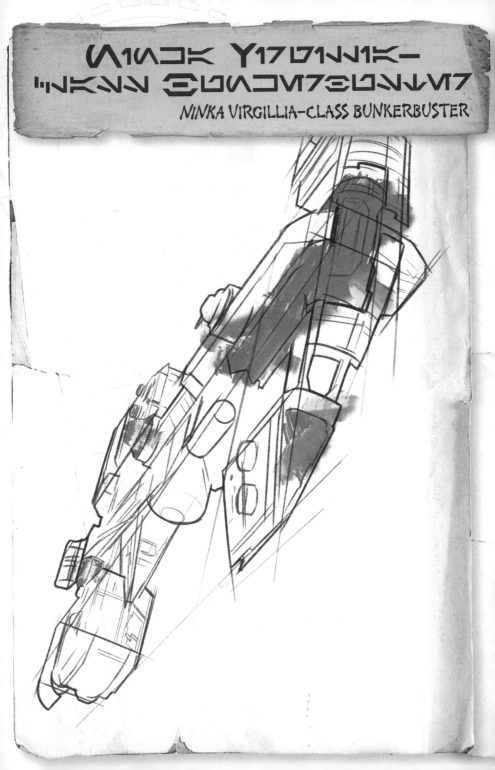

NINKA VIRGILLIA-CLASS BUNKERBUSTER

Paige and the other bomber crews would cover our base's evacuation, but Holdo asked me to stay aboard the _Ninka_ and help adapt my baffler for use on other ships. She promised that when we reached D'Qar I'd transfer to the _Raddus_, General Organa's flagship, and reunite with Paige.

I didn't want to do it. I hated to be apart from my sister. But I knew had to follow Holdo's orders.

Poe Dameron, one of the heroic X-wing pilots from the battle at Starkiller, led the bombers into battle to buy some time so all of the Resistance crew members could escape from the base on D'Qar. They attacked a First Order Siege Dreadnought, but *Cobalt Hammer* was the only bomber to reach its target and drop its payload. Its bombs destroyed the Dreadnought, though, which allowed the rest of the Resistance escape.

But *Cobalt Hammer* couldn't escape the explosion. That's how I lost Paige. That's how she died. Fossil had been monitoring the battle from the bridge and she told me that my sister was the only crew member alive when the bomber reached its target. That means it was Paige who dropped the bombs and saved everyone. Then, Fossil gave me an old REBEL RING, to honor the fact that Paige had died like she had lived—as a hero.

I DIDN'T WANT A RING. I WANTED PAIGE.

I wish it had all just been a dream. It was a nightmare, really. But I knew that it was real. This was my new reality. A life without Paige. It hurt so much.

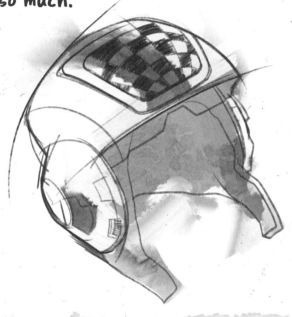

Why did I tell Holdo I'd stay aboard the *Ninka?* Because I wanted to make the First Order pay, that's why. I wasn't a great pilot or an expert gunner like Paige, but working on bafflers could keep our pilots and gunners safe and let them shoot down more First Order fighters. Didn't I have a responsibility to do that?

I was thinking about other people too. About Reeve Panzoro, a freedom fighter we met on Atterra Bravo. He didn't want to be separated from his grandmother, but knew he had to if he was going to accomplish his mission. And there was Cat, another flight engineer in *Cobalt Squadron*. During our Atterra missions, Fossil asked me to switch places with another bomber's flight engineer. When I said I couldn't fly without my sister, Cat volunteered to switch instead. A day later, TIE fighters blew the other bomber out of space. I felt like Cat died because I'd been selfish.

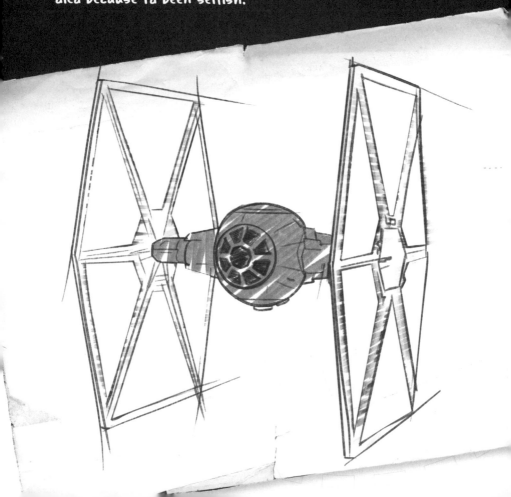

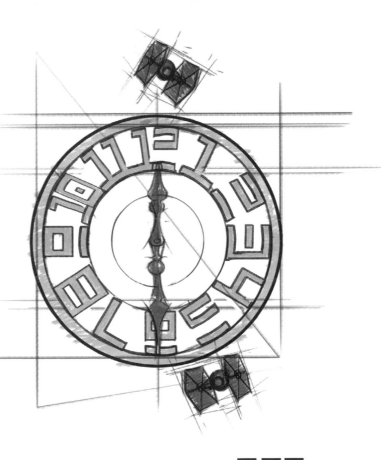

I thought about all those things and said I'd help Holdo, even though it was the last thing in the galaxy I wanted to do.

I wish I'd said no, but then I reminded myself of the job that my sister and I left Hays Minor to do: fight the First Order. Paige would want me to keep fighting. So I'll do that the best I can, in memory of my family, and my friends aboard *Cobalt Hammer*. And Cat, and all the people at Hosnian Prime. And so many others.

■■■ SERVING THE RESISTANCE

ꓥꓦ∫ꓬꓴ(ꓥꓴ∫ ꓥ∫ꓦⅠ ꓮꓦꓲꓓꓴ∫ꓤꓦ(ꓥ¬∫ꓦ

The *Ninka* wasn't new to me: our StarFortress bombers used the ship as a base for missions against pirates in the Cassander sector. She—the *Ninka* is always referred to as "she" or "her," even though lots of people consider that old-fashioned—was the first real warship Paige and I had ever been on.

The *Ninka's* a bunkerbuster with a hammerhead bow covered with bomb ports. She was built to target the Empire's underground bases. Her first officer, a Sullustan named Gibs Nibbet, told me the ship could crack open a small moon and swore that if the *Ninka* had been at Starkiller Base, the Resistance wouldn't have needed starfighters. Everyone who works on board the *Ninka* is proud of their tough little ship.

As for the *Ninka's* commander, well, that's interesting. Before the Cassander missions, Fossil warned me that Vice Admiral Holdo didn't look or act like other Resistance officers. She was right. Holdo is tall and graceful, and her boldly colored clothing matches her bright hair and eyes.

Sometimes Holdo says strange things too. When Paige and I first met her, she noted that we were from Otomok and said she found ice amazing. It could be clear as glass while hard as steel, able to resist everything except time . . . which would turn it into harmless water.

"Isn't that curious?" she asked.

Pae-Pae didn't know what to say. I said I'd never thought about it that way, but, wow, was that ever true.

After my sister died, and I was waiting for a shuttle to arrive and take me to the *Raddus*, I heard my name and looked up to see Holdo had come to find me. She told me that Paige would want me to live, not to grieve.

I told her I planned to live and that I also planned to honor my sister by striking back against the First Order. By making them hurt . . . hurt like I was hurting.

Holdo shook her head. She said *that* was grieving, not living. Then she said that if I did that, I would make the mistake of not having anything to live for except my sister.

"That's your mission, then, Rose Tico," she said. "Not bafflers and mechanical whatsits. Figure out what you want to live for."

I knew Holdo was just trying to be kind, but she never really knew me or my sister that well, so who was she to tell me not to grieve? I was ready to return to the *Raddus* and report back to General Leia again. She had welcomed Paige and me with open arms when we had first arrived on D'Qar.

But the *Ninka* crew had been nice, too.

Holdo had asked me to explain the baffler technology to her boffins—that's what bomber crews call scientist types—so they could share the design with the rest of the fleet.

Holdo's boffins worked in a clubhouse near the *Ninka's* bow that contained a junkyard worth of stuff the Resistance had scrounged. All boffins are a bit weird—I learned that in *Cobalt Squadron*—but Mersh, Forzee, Timo, and Fasca made Holdo seem normal.

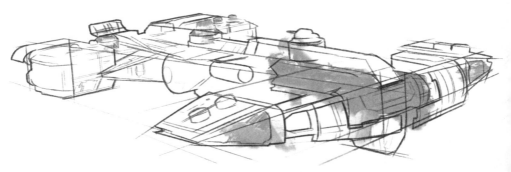

■■■

    Mersh Pellus is an ancient human who just looked confused when I asked him where his homeworld was, then he pointed to a hammock tied up over the junk pile. He has a long white beard and an ancient pair of manual magni-lenses that he's blind without. Mersh is brilliant. I'd only been explaining my baffler for about 15 seconds when he nodded and predicted three mistakes I'd made. But he's so absent-minded that Holdo programmed a butler droid, SE-4Z, to follow him around. Forzee has two jobs: to remind Mersh that his goggles are on top of his head so he won't spend an hour looking for them, and to stop him from entering the bridge during battles to explain his latest idea.

Forzee once served the emir of Grand Tharkand, and never misses a chance to compare the Tharkandian royal palace with the mess that surrounds him now. To keep from going crazy, he's loaded engineering textbooks and databases of inventions into his memory, and consults them whenever the team gets a new problem to work on. The others ridicule whatever he tells them, but then when they think Forzee isn't listening they quietly do whatever he suggested. And Forzee's always listening.

The third member of Holdo's team, Timo Hoxwa, is a massive Lotran who is almost as smart as Mersh and even better at solving problems because she actually listens instead of getting lost in dreamland. Timo rarely speaks, but when she does the others stop bickering and listen.

Fasca Tiradé is the fourth member, a Zilkin no bigger than your hand. I'd never heard of a Zilkin, and assumed Fasca was Timo's pet. Big mistake. Fasca's a foul-mouthed creature, able to insult you in about two dozen languages.

I HADN'T THOUGHT MY
BAFFLERS WERE A BIG
DEAL. I FIGURED LOTS OF
PEOPLE ON D'QAR COULD
HAVE COME UP WITH A
BETTER IDEA. BUT WHEN
MERSH SAID I'D DONE
IMPRESSIVE WORK,
I FINALLY BELIEVED IT.
I HAD BLUSHED AND TIMO
CLAPPED ME ON THE
BACK SO HARD
SHE ALMOST KNOCKED
ME OVER.

I'LL MISS MERSH'S
BOFFINS. FOR A WHILE
THEY FELT A BIT LIKE
FAMILY, AND THAT MADE
EVERYTHING I WAS
STRUGGLING WITH HURT
A LITTLE LESS.

I was in such a daze that I doubted I could fly, but all that simulator time must have paid off: I qualified for three classes of loadlifters and every shuttle in the fleet. When I got the results, all could I think about was how Paige would have hugged me and told me how proud she was.

But there were no ships to fly. No one seemed to know what was going on with the fleet. So I was assigned to maintenance work, checking airlocks and escape pods, air scrubbers and coolant reservoirs.

That's droidwork, and I guess I should have been angry that the Resistance seemed to have forgotten about me. I mean, I'd gone from programming bafflers to checking magno-latches. But I didn't really care. It was a relief to shuffle along gloomy corridors by myself, and the *Raddus* has *lots* of corridors.

THEN EVERYTHING WENT CRAZY

Without warning, First Order torpedoes hit the *Raddus's* bridge. For the first hour or so the ship was full of rumors, each worse than the last. The truth turned out to be nearly as bad: the entire command crew had been killed except for General Organa, and medical droids were trying to keep her alive.

And who was her replacement as the Resistance commander? None other than Vice Admiral Holdo!

Escape pods started launching . . . people were deserting the ship! An officer gave me an electro-prod and orders to stun any unauthorized personnel near the pod bays. I was happy to do it. Those cowards were running away from the very fleet my sister had given her life to save. They were traitors not just to the Resistance but also to Paige's memory.

WHICH IS WHERE FINN COMES INTO MY STORY.

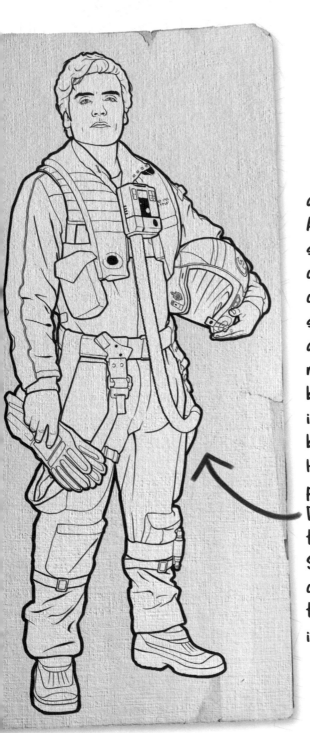

Pae-Pae had told me about Finn after the Atterra mission. She said he'd been one of the orphans sent off to First Order space and turned into a soldier without a name. That kind of brainwashing is almost impossible to shake, but Finn had done it. He'd abandoned his post to rescue Poe Dameron, then joined the mission to destroy Starkiller Base, serving on the commando team that brought down its shields.

That's a hero, Paige told me—
someone who does what's right
and doesn't run away. And he'd
done it despite years of being
fed the First Order's lies. If
someone could do that, Paige
said, there was hope for the
galaxy after all. She hoped one
day we'd get to meet him.

And OK, when I met Finn
the first thing I noticed was
that he certainly looked like
a hero, except for the fact
that he was sneaking into an
escape pod with a canvas bag!
So I gave him a blast from
a fully loaded electro-prod.
That's enough charge to stun
a Wookiee, so Finn hit the
ground and I started dragging
him to the brig. And man was
he heavy! Whatever he's got
to say about the First Order,
they sure didn't starve him.

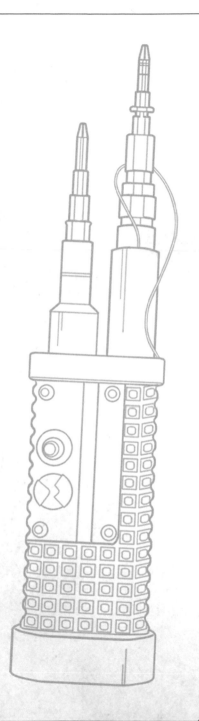

Finn woke up and started rambling. He kept talking about his friend Rey. He had to leave to find Rey. Rey this and Rey that. I had heard about Rey before—she was another hero from the battle on Starkiller. But I didn't care what Finn had to say about her. It wasn't going to stop me from turning him in for desertion. BUT THEN HE SAID SOMETHING THAT MADE ME RECONSIDER.

Finn told me the First Order had tracked us through *hyperspace*, something I'd always heard was impossible! We were just out of range of the First Order's guns, but with no chance of escape. Eventually we'd run out of fuel, the First Order would blast us into atoms, and that would be the end of the Resistance.

That explained why people were willing to take their chances in an escape pod. But I got interested in the puzzle.

I don't know how the First Order finally solved all the problems with hyperspace tracking. But the principle isn't complicated: a hyperspace tracker is just a really powerful version of an active tracker, which warships use for everything from targeting to communications.

I know all about active trackers, because I spent lots of boring hours maintaining them on our bombers.

I made some diagrams, but the short version is you only have one active tracker running at a time to avoid interference. And because active trackers are so important, they have dedicated circuit breakers to make sure they don't shut off during a fight.

You won't find dedicated circuits on a ship's bridge, but down below decks where people like me work. And Finn, it so happened, knew where they were located on the First Order flagship.

So all we had to do was get aboard the First Order flagship, shut off the hyperspace tracker's circuit breaker, and tell the Resistance fleet to jump before the First Order could switch to a different tracker.

EASY, RIGHT?

ACTIVE TRACKER

ONE STARFORTRESS the illuminator—turns on active tracking, using it to gather and map target data, then transmitting that information to the other bombers on the hop.

ACTIVE-TRACKER SCANNING puts out A LOT of energy. If you use multiple trackers at once, it's really hard to avoid interference — which will make your data useless.

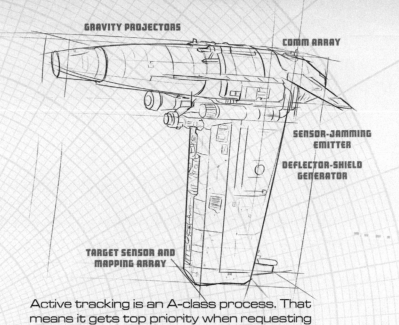

GRAVITY PROJECTORS

COMM ARRAY

SENSOR-JAMMING EMITTER

DEFLECTOR-SHIELD GENERATOR

TARGET SENSOR AND MAPPING ARRAY

Active tracking is an A-class process. That means it gets top priority when requesting computing power from a ship's systems.

DEDICATED CIRCUIT BREAKER FOR ACTIVE TRACKING ARRAY

FLIGHT ENGINEER'S STATION

TARGET SENSOR AND MAPPING ARRAY ACTIVE TRACKER

Every A-class process also has its own dedicated circuit. You don't want your targeting computer to go dark because the climate-control system's overloaded!

Except we needed a really good codebreaker to figure out the clearance codes to get us through the security perimeter. Which is how we wound up talking to this strange friend of Finn's named Maz, who told us the man we needed to break the code could be found in the glamorous gambling city of Canto Bight on Cantonica.

We also needed permission to go on this crazy trip. I wish Paige could have seen her kid sister talking to the best star pilot in the Resistance.

Poe Dameron thought our plan was insane. He also thought Holdo would hate the idea. That's why he agreed to help—turns out Poe doesn't like Holdo very much.

While Poe distracted Holdo, we slipped away from the fleet in a shuttle. With my brand-new pilot certification, I'm taking us to Cantonica, where a man with a red plom bloom in his lapel—according to Maz, at least—may or may not be waiting for us. (I didn't even know what a plom bloom was until I looked it up a moment ago.)

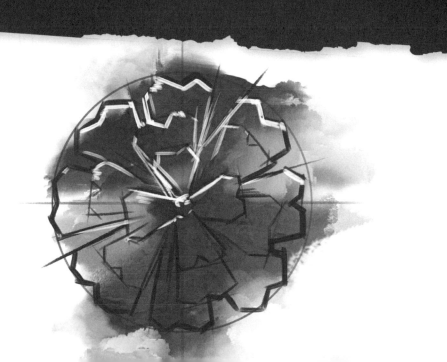

IN THE PAST FEW HOURS, I'VE FIGURED OUT A LITTLE OF WHAT MAKES FINN TICK. HE'S IN LOVE WITH HIS FRIEND REY. THAT'S WHY HE WENT TO STARKILLER BASE. IT HAD NOTHING TO DO WITH THE RESISTANCE OR GALACTIC FREEDOM. HE JUST REALLY WANTED TO HELP HIS FRIEND.

I guess I can understand that. Paige and I would have done anything for each other, after all. But not at the expense of so many other lives. That's the part that really frustrates me. It's like Finn hasn't noticed anything else that's happening in the galaxy.

Maybe I'm just jealous. Or sad. All I know is Finn still has someone he'd do anything for. All I've got is the Resistance, and I don't know if that's enough to keep me going. But for now, it will have to be. Finn's best chance to save his friend is to stop the First Order, which is also my best chance to save our fleet.

SO I GUESS WE'RE A TEAM NOW.

Poe's BB unit stowed away on our shuttle! Apparently this mission wasn't crazy enough when it was just a love-struck First Order deserter and a maintenance tech with delusions of grandeur. We also needed a crazy droid.

■■■ CANTO BIGHT

IT HASN'T BEEN THAT LONG SINCE MY LAST ENTRY, BUT I'M . . . EXHAUSTED, OVERWHELMED, YOU NAME IT.

As for our mission, well, it's taken an interesting turn. I don't know if this adventure will end with me and Finn saving the fleet, or spending the rest of our lives in a First Order prison.

Cantonica is a desert world. The only reason to go there is to visit Canto Bight, a resort where it practically rains credits. Everyone in the casinos was wearing furs, fancy clothes, jewels, cybernetic implants, and things I couldn't even recognize.

They were risking a normal person's lifetime's pay on a single hand of Zinbiddle cards, toss of the dice, or spin of the jubilee wheel. I HATED THE PLACE.

Lots of Canto Bight's workers can't even afford to live there. They take shuttles down from one of the grimy industrial moons, or live ten to a room in some filthy hovel in Old Town. The boardwalk along the beach is lovely, but the sea is fake. Rich tourists wanted water to sparkle in the moonlight during a romantic stroll, so Canto Bight's barons built them a sea.

I wanted to drag all those rich beings away from the Hazard Toss tables and the gill-flush saunas and demand to know if they'd missed that an entire solar system had been incinerated. Or that every day the First Order was occupying new planets. But then I realized I was the naïve one. They knew what was happening on other planets. They just didn't care. They had enough credits to stay one step ahead of any war—or to buy protection from a new regime.

GAMES OF CHANCE

And I figured that out before I realized how many of them were arms dealers—the same scum Paige and I used to see back home. I overheard them laughing while talking about First Order fleet deployments and New Republic calls for aid and independent star systems building up their defenses. The idea of a new galaxy-wide war didn't bother them in the least. It excited them.

THAT'S WHEN
I GOT MAD.

And it made me even madder seeing how much Finn seemed to enjoy being there. Maybe I shouldn't be too hard on him—if he ever visited a nice place as a stormtrooper his job was to blow it up— but seeing a goofy grin on that heroic face irritated me. And if Finn wasn't drooling on the casino tables, he was mooning about Rey . . . how she was a great pilot and he knew she'd be a great Jedi and he couldn't wait to see her again.

Rey **Rey Rey.**

IT MADE ME WANT TO SCREAM. LIKE HE KNOWS ANYTHING.

Still, Paige would have liked him. She would have said he had a good heart. And she wouldn't have been wrong.

BUT ENOUGH ABOUT FINN.

We were looking for Maz's master codebreaker—the man with the red plom bloom—and eventually we found him. I wish I could tell you about him and his ingenious plan to infiltrate the First Order and how well it's going, but that's not what happened.

Because just when we found him, the Canto Bight police found us!

Turns out you can't land a shuttle on a Canto Bight beach, even if the fate of the galaxy might depend on it, and even though the planet's nothing but sand. They have stupid laws against that, and stupid police officers with nothing better to do but enforce those stupid laws.

So, we did find the man with the red plom bloom, but the next thing we knew we were being hauled off to jail. Great plan so far.

FATHIERS

Remember how I wrote that Paige loved all animals—even Otomok slime molds? Well, her favorite animals in the entire galaxy were fathiers. And Finn and I wouldn't have escaped Canto Bight without meeting a herd of them.

When we were little, Pae-Pae would watch holo-documentaries about fathiers—dopey thrillers in which poor girls trained fathiers to become champion racers, and all the high-stakes fathier races; Caprioril Downs, the Wheel Invitational, and the Kushal Vogh Promenade. We thought the betting thing was strange though, because watching fathiers run was exciting enough.

WHAT STRUCK ME ABOUT FATHIERS WAS THEY LOOKED REALLY ODD STANDING STILL. YOU NEEDED TO SEE THEM IN MOTION TO NOTICE HOW PERFECTLY AERODYNAMIC THEIR EARS ARE, OR TO ADMIRE THE GRACE AND POWER OF THE MUSCLES IN THEIR LEGS AND FLANKS AND BACKS.

CANTO BIGHT

FATHIER RACES

Tonight's Program

BROUGHT TO YOU BY ALL ACES CRYSTALMEAD.
IT'S ALWAYS A WINNING HAND!

Your Field for Tonight's Fifth Race

KESSEL RUNNER

3   Br   C

1

1•4•P

ARCA YROCA
BIG STURG GANNA

Hydian Dreams
out of Distant Star

SHIFTING SANDS

5   Pa   S

2

D•2•2

PINRADO NORZA
BIG STURG GANNA

Virtuous Velocity
out of Imperial

BONADAN STAR

4   Wh   G

3

3•5•3

**TURCOTTE
BEL MONT**
PAKKERD RACING

Etti Express
out of Farana's Folly

VERMILION

3   Ch   F

4

1•1•U

KRIN KALLIBIN
FIBS NIBBELT

Crimson Pavane
out of Cinnabar

MYNOCK MINUTE

3   Br   C

5

5•6•6

XIS GABBARD
UBBLA MOLLBRO

Doonium Strike
out of Take Flight

HY-STEPPING

6   Bl   S

6

4•8•7

HANNA DEVALLT
DEFANCIO STORSILT

Hydian Dreams
out of Solar Promenade

HOW TO READ YOUR RACING FORM	SILKS PHOTO	FATHIER NAME	POST#
		Age Color Class	
	JOCKEY OWNER	Sire Dam	Last 3 Results

Paige hated it when fathier jockeys used whips—lots of our make-believe adventures were about freeing abused fathiers from wicked racetrack owners. Sometimes, when I was wedged beside Paige in our bomber's ball turret, I'd say that after the war was over we'd buy a stable on some sunny planet where fathiers would have all the grass they wanted and all the space they needed to run. Paige would smile and squeeze my hand, and for a few seconds it felt like the war was far away.

When I saw fathiers thunder past on the Canto Bight racetrack, I thought I was dreaming. I hadn't really imagined that I'd see one someday, but there they were, so much bigger and more beautiful than on a holo-screen.

I only caught a glimpse of them before we got tossed in jail. Someone else was in our cell though—a grimy thief named DJ, who bragged that he was an ace codebreaker.

(I SURE HOPE HE'S TELLING THE TRUTH ABOUT THAT.)

Then when BB-8 tried to rescue us (that droid is as brave as it is crazy), DJ used the distraction to pop the cell door open and stroll out of prison.

There was no way out for us and the guards were closing in, so we went the only place we could . . . down through a grate and into the sewer tunnel beneath the jail. It was dark down there and it smelled terrible, but fortunately Cantonica's a pretty dry planet, so we didn't have to wade through anything disgusting.

The problem was we had a choice of directions, and we disagreed on which way to go. Finn said the tunnel was slightly inclined and we should go up in case the sewer emptied into the sea. I said it smelled worse in that direction, and we should go in the direction that didn't stink.

Do you know how we settled it? With a round of wonga winga cingee wooze, which I guess Finn learned before going off to stormtrooper school. He won, and so we went up, toward the bad smell. The tunnel ended in a ladder, and we climbed it and found ourselves in a stable, of all things. Right in front of us was a fathier. There were raggedy kids taking care of the animals, and I saw one of them was about to hit the alarm. So I broke one of the first rules of the Resistance and told him who we were.

I'm not sure he believed it, but I also had the ring Fossil had given me in Paige's memory. I gave it to the stable boy, and he looked at it a moment, then promised to help us.

I spoke just enough of his language to understand he was telling us to climb on the fathier matriarch's back. She was huge and warm, and I could feel her lungs expanding and contracting beneath me, like a giant living engine. Finn was terrified, but not me. I could feel the fathier trembling, but she wasn't frightened. SHE WANTED OUT.

And that's what we did. The stable kids opened all twenty stalls, so every fathier in the place followed the matriarch. OH HOW I MISSED PAIGE IN THAT MOMENT. What she wouldn't have done to see them. They couldn't even lie down to sleep in those stalls, the poor things, but when they figured out they'd get a chance to run their ears perked up and they started to paw at the ground.

While the kids all cheered, our line of fathiers smashed past the police and started racing around the track in the empty stadium. Finn was hanging on behind me for dear life and yelling which way to go, but the matriarch was in charge. We were just along for the ride.

When our fathier saw police speeders closing in, she snorted and smashed right through a window and out onto the casino floor, with the whole herd following her. I swear she saw a chance to bust that place up and was happy to take it. They stampeded through Canto Bight, wrecking cafes and trampling speeders and making rich goons dive under tables. It was glorious. Then we got out onto the beach, where they could really run.

The matriarch ran out into the flatlands, but the police were everywhere. Our fathier was fast, moving like a tremendous machine, but there was no way even she could outrun a police speeder. I realized they were herding us to the edge of a cliff. We quickly dismounted and I patted the matriarch and urged her to get out of there before the police caught up to us.

I was convinced that by failing to recruit the Master Codebreaker we'd blown our last chance to save the Resistance. But part of me was happy anyway. An hour earlier I'd been someone who could only dream of seeing a fathier one day, and now I knew what it was like to ride one at top speed.

It hurt that Paige hadn't been there to see it too. But I also knew she would have been happier for me than she was sad for herself. Paige had always wanted to see fathiers with her kid sister, and that would never happen. But she still would have clapped her hands with glee to know what I'd done. Before the police arrived, I touched my medallion and silently told Paige that fathiers were even more beautiful than we'd imagined.

I had to laugh at Finn, though. He thought that DJ was using his own luxury yacht to sneak up on the First Order. Hey, you big goof—he stole it.

If only Finn would quit talking to that lowlife, though. I heard DJ tell him that the galaxy's a big machine that chews people up, and the way to win is never to pick a side but just to look for opportunities to profit. DJ isn't even his name, but a nickname—it stands for Don't Join.

I WORRY FINN MIGHT LISTEN TO HIM.

After all, when I first saw Finn, he was trying to run away from the Resistance. I've heard him talk about leaving one army and not wanting to get caught up in another one, which sure sounds like Don't Join to me. And Finn . . . well, he's *impressionable*. That's not a surprise though. Not really. He was raised by crazy soldiers and never had parents or an older sibling to help him make the right decisions, like I did. I mean, he never even had a name until Poe gave him one, just a number. Imagine going through life named FN-2187.

I remember Paige telling me I needed to work on not letting my anger get the best of me. Maybe that's what I'm doing. Maybe Finn and I aren't so different. And if Finn's not so different from DJ, maybe all three of us are more similar than I'd like to think.

DJ's pretty simple to figure out—he's only out for himself.

Finn's in love with a girl from Jakku that he barely knows. Which makes me want to strangle him, but it's more than DJ's ever done or felt for anybody.

■ ■ ■

So what about me? I wound up in the Resistance by accident. My parents sent me and my sister to them. Now my parents and Paige are gone, and so is my home. What's left for me?

Assuming I live through whatever's next, I have to figure that out. I have to figure a lot of things out.

Right after Paige died, I wanted to make the First Order hurt—the way they've made me and so many other people hurt. But a funny thing happened after the fathiers rampaged through the casino.

At the time, I loved crashing through that beautiful place. But thinking back on it now, I just feel empty. The fathiers are back in their stalls, and probably some of them got hurt by running off with us. The stable kids definitely got in trouble for helping us. And I'm sure the casino bosses just fixed up the damage and are raking in credits again.

SO WHAT WAS THE POINT?

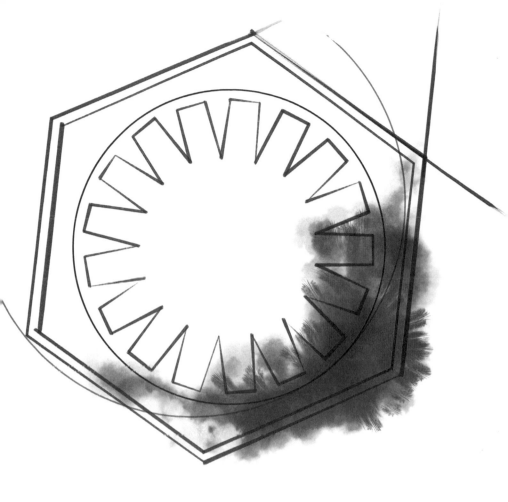

I'm not saying I'm going to become like DJ. He's worked so hard to not care about anything that now he wouldn't be *able* to care if he wanted to. But all of a sudden I have to wonder:

IS THIS FIGHT JUST TOO BIG FOR ME?

■■■ AGAINST THE FIRST ORDER

That last thing I wrote feels like a long time ago, even if it was only a couple of days. I am not sure how much more I'll be able to write—they tell me I have to rest and heal. I'm listening, if only to keep Finn from going crazy if I try to sit up.

So I'll make this short. Let me tell you about the *Supremacy*—the ship that slime mold DJ called "Snoke's boudoir."

Growing up on Hays Minor, I rarely saw a ship bigger than an atmospheric hopper. The junky supply ship Paige and I rode from Otomok to Botajef seemed huge to me.

The *Ninka* was bigger, and the *Raddus* really was a giant. But nothing prepared me for the sight of Snoke's flagship. It's fully 60 kilometers from wingtip to wingtip. I didn't need to feel embarrassed for gaping like some yokel from the Outer Rim. As far as I know, no one's ever seen a ship that big—not in the history of the galaxy.

DJ knew the codes to get us through the *Supremacy's* security perimeter, and attached our ship to that monster's hull. Turned out he told the truth about that. We snuck aboard and found ourselves in a laundry room. It was full of First Order uniforms—exactly what we needed to sneak through a giant warship full of people trying to kill us.

Compared with the Resistance, the First Order's technology was amazing. Everything was shiny and new, instead of patched together. On the *Supremacy*, we were surrounded by the quiet hum of a ship in perfect working order—nothing was rattling or coughing, blackened by smoke, or discolored by corrosion.

The people were shiny and new too—uniforms clean and perfectly fitted, boots polished, rank badges straight. (More than one officer did a double take to see the scruffy DJ in uniform.) But there was something dead in their eyes, like they were machines. They sort of are. That's what the First Order does to kids like Finn. It breaks them down and tries to make them like droids whose only purpose is to serve the First Order's agenda.

LAUNDRY AND VALET SERVICES

Items must be in your tagged bundle and available for droid pickup by 1000, 1800 or 0200 depending on your duty shift. Failure to adhere to standard pickup times will result in demerits. Failure to properly fill out this form, including inaccurate specification of damage to items, will result in demerits and/or additional corrective action.

No.	Item Description	Dam.	No.	Item Description	Dam.
	Cap			Training Shirt	
	Tunic			Training Shorts	
	Trousers			Training Unitard	
	Gloves			Training Socks	
	Socks			Greatcoat	
	Dress cap			Watch Cap	
	Dress Tunic			Service Sweater	
	Dress Trousers			Inclement Weather Poncho	
	Dress Gloves			Brassiere	
	Cape/Cloak			Underwear	
	Nonstandard Item			Belt	
	Boots			Nonstandard Footwear	

- Each nonstandard item must be accompanied by a Laundry/Valet Waiver 44-B.
- Each damaged item must be accompanied by a Damaged Item/Equipment Explanation Form 31-C.
- Each garment has an identification nano-chip assigned to its owner. No other officer's garments should be in your bundle. Exceptions must be accompanied by a Laundry/Valet Waiver 44-H.
- Rank cylinders, datapads and sidearms should never be placed in a bundle. Any rank cylinder discovered during laundry/valet operations will be reset and result in demerits and/or additional corrective action.

PERSONAL CLEANLINESS IS THE FOUNDATION OF ORGANIZATIONAL PURITY

The galaxy has BILLIONS and BILLIONS of unique worlds that are homes to species of every shape and size and animals that not even my sister could have imagined. When I think about all that I'm overcome by how beautiful and exciting and inspiring it is, but the First Order just sees chaos, disorder, and threats. They want to turn all those worlds and species and animals into fuel for a war machine that will stomp everything flat and make it the same.

And there we were in the heart of that war machine. Finn had served aboard the *Supremacy*, and told me that it was built to be not just a massive warship but also as an assembly line for weapons and vehicles and a training center for cadets.

It's weird to think that giant ship is gone now . . . But I'm getting ahead of myself again. And I need to sleep some more before Finn peeks in and gives me another lecture.

That's better. Or at least
it's a little better—everything
hurts, and this broken-down
freighter doesn't exactly
have state-of-the-art
medical facilities.

Back to the *Supremacy*.

Our destination was the
circuit breakers in
tracking control. If we shut
those down, we'd give
the Resistance fleet a six-
minute window in which it
could jump to safety.

Finn, DJ, and I had our
uniforms, and BB-8 to help
us find our way, and I was
pretty sure we could shut
down the tracker if we got to
that circuit breaker. But the
ship was filled with officers
and stormtroopers, and every
step we took I worried that DJ
would panic and give the game
away . . . or I would mess up.

I wasn't worried about Finn, though. The moment he put on that First Order uniform, it was like I could see the officer he might have become. It scared me a bit to imagine how just a little change might have turned a good man into the total opposite. But I could also see his bravery and his determination, which impressed me even more because he was back among people who would consider him a traitor.

■■■

What I didn't know was that our mission was already doomed. I had no idea that DJ had sold us out to Captain Phasma and the First Order before we ever left Cantonica. I should have known when he gave me my medallion back—the first kind gesture I'd ever seen him make. I guess he felt guilty, which he should have, because he led us right into the First Order's trap.

After the First Order paid DJ for delivering us to them, this arrogant general named Hux, came to gloat over our impending deaths. He pointed at my medallion and said it brought back memories—and then he dared to call my people vermin.

So I bit his finger—hard. Not because I thought it could save us, but because I wanted to leave a mark on him—a scar that would make him remember Otomok, and me.

(BY THE WAY, HE TASTED TERRIBLE.)

THE GENERAL ORDERED THAT WE BE EXECUTED BY STORMTROOPERS WITH LASER AXES. I FOUND MYSELF ON MY KNEES, PREPARED TO DIE . . . AND YET I FELT STRANGELY CALM. AND IT WAS BECAUSE I WAS LOOKING AT FINN.

Maybe we hadn't met under the best of circumstances—you don't usually stun someone right off the bat—but I suddenly realized that I trusted him, and that he had risked his life for me. All the time I'd thought I was alone in the galaxy without my sister, but Finn had been there beside me. I didn't want to die, but there were worse ways to go than next to someone I'd come to love.

Except we didn't die. This time it was Holdo who saved us—well, her and Poe's crazy droid again.

The *Raddus* was all that was left of the fleet, and its fuel tanks were almost empty. Holdo ordered everyone to squeeze into the transports I'd helped her tech team outfit with bafflers. Their destination was Crait, a long-abandoned rebel base, and the plan was to hole up and call for help from General Organa's allies in the Outer Rim.

   But Holdo hadn't told anybody that plan . . . or that she would remain aboard the *Raddus* and draw the First Order's fire.

   When the First Order started blasting the transports, Holdo used the last of the *Raddus's* fuel to jump to hyperspace, on a course that punched right *through* Snoke's flagship, tearing it in half, and took out several other Star Destroyers as well. Fortunately, the *Supremacy* was big enough that Finn and I weren't killed by the impact, but we were left aboard a chunk of a ruined ship adrift in space.

I was wrong about Holdo. She sacrificed herself to save all our lives. I just wish she'd trusted more people with her plan. It must have been so lonely, remaining silent while people like me and Poe suspected her of being a coward or even a traitor.

When the *Raddus* ripped through the *Supremacy* everything was thrown into chaos, which gave BB-8 a chance to take control of a scout walker and open fire on the troops holding us prisoner. Finn and I stole a First Order shuttle and escaped with BB-8.

We could have taken our stolen shuttle anywhere, but we headed where we knew we belonged—with the Resistance, on Crait. We got there just before they closed the shield doors of the old rebel base, but the doors weren't enough to protect us.

The First Order sent down TIE fighters, and the heavy walkers, and began dragging a cannon across the salt plains—one big enough to blow the shield doors to atoms. The only weapons we could find in the base were some heavy blasters and a few rickety ski speeders that looked like they wouldn't even run, let alone be able to do anything against walkers.

■■■

People looked like they wanted to crawl into the caverns and hide until the First Order dragged them out. But then Finn started talking. He said that if we could take out that cannon, we could buy ourselves more time. He insisted we had allies, and they'd get our message and help us. Anyway, what were we going to do? Not fight?

This was the same Finn that I'd found running away, who'd thought about his one friend instead of all the other people in danger. And he'd said "we"—not "you crazy maniacs I need to get away from as quickly as possible." He said "we," and he meant it. And I was part of that "we"—a feeling I hadn't had about the Resistance since I last saw Paige.

We got several ski speeders working and raced across the salt plains, kicking up red tails of dirt behind us. I was trying to remember my airspeeder simulations. I worried that I'd crash a hundred meters from the base, and that the first blast from one of those walkers would turn me to ash.

BUT I REALIZED I WAS HAPPY.

Not happy like in the traditional sense, because I was terrified every single second. But I finally knew what I was fighting *for,* and I believed in it with my whole heart. I realized something else, too: what Paige had tried to teach me, when she'd warned me about letting hate dominate my emotions. And it was the same thing Holdo had tried to tell me when she said I needed to figure out what to live for.

I still wanted to stop the First Order, but now I wasn't thinking about revenge for Otomok, my parents, or my sister. Instead, I was thinking about the lives we'd save by stopping them. Revenge, I realized, would never be enough. I'd never stop being angry and would wind up empty—empty and twisted into something I'd never wanted to be.

We had to fight on Crait, and the fighting is far from over.

BUT WE WON'T WIN BY FIGHTING WHAT WE HATE. RATHER, WE'LL WIN BY SAVING WHAT WE LOVE.

That's what I figured out, piloting a ski speeder I thought might fall apart even without a walker shooting it. And so when Finn went crazy and tried to sacrifice himself to stop the First Order's cannon from firing, I stopped him instead. I blasted his ski speeder and knocked it away from the cannon and out of danger.

It worked, except for the part where I smashed up my speeder and myself. I don't remember much after that. My head was pounding and everything hurt, but I know I told Finn what I'd figured out. And then—because the guy has a way of missing the obvious—I kissed him.

And then I woke up aboard this junk heap of a freighter. What's left of the Resistance, as far as I can tell, is aboard this one small ship. But we've got General Organa. And Poe. And Finn. And Finn's friend, the famous Rey. The others say she lifted a mountain out of the way so we could escape.

VULPTEX PROFILE

FIELD NOTES ON THE VUL

DR. PAQIN MESOLI, STAFF XENOBIOLOGIST, NUPAYUNI MINING (

The vulptex (plural: vulptices) dwells in highland caves and canyons. Vulptices are omnivorous, digging beneath the salt crust for burrowing mammals and tubers. Though not sentient, they are intelligent creatures that form strong family/pack bonds and hunt cooperatively.

The vulptex has excellent low-light vision and keen senses. Further observations are required to determine whether it hunts primarily by sight, hearing, sense of smell, or some combination of the three. It may also be sensitive to magnetic fields. Investigation needed.

Unique crystalline bristles/spines serve as protection against predators' attacks. I suspect – though I can't confirm – that vulptices also use their bristles to communicate, shaking them or brushing against stone to create distinctive sound patterns.

⊙ POSSIBLE TO DOMESTICATE THEM?

⊙ MIXED RECORD OF SUCCESS WITH OTHER CANIDS.

⊙ SUMMER DENS BENEATH SALT CRUST?

⊙ WINTER DENS IN CAVERNS?

Vulptices typically live in groups of three to four families with as many as 10 animals per family, but I have observed these groups come together in larger social structures, with as many as 100 vulptices sharing a particularly desirable den.

Flexible bodies allow vulptices to squeeze into crevices that seem far too small for passage. They use their facial bristles/whiskers to gauge whether they can fit into a space.

Rey is very interesting. It's like her mind is very far away, and she's looking at something the rest of us can't see. And whatever that something is, it's so much bigger than all of us, and maybe all of this.

Which reminds me of the last entry I recorded before we—Leia, Poe, Finn and a few others—had escaped through the back of the old rebel base on Crait by following strange crystal foxes (called vulptices) through a winding cave. And I heard that the famous Rey had even moved boulders out of the way using the Force so everyone could reach the *Falcon* and escape. Someone must have have carried me on board. I hope it was Finn...

Back then, I worried that this fight was too big for me. And I still feel pretty small compared with everything that's going on around us. But I'm at peace with that.

I can't take on the First Order all by myself. Neither can Finn or General Organa or even Rey. None of us can.

All we can do is our best, for each other.

When Paige died, it comforted me that her sacrifice had let the Resistance fleet escape. When it turned out the First Order could track us through hyperspace, I felt like my sister had died for nothing—like the First Order had taken not just her life but also her right to be called a hero.

Then, when the First Order captured us aboard the *Supremacy*, I felt like I'd let everybody down . . . not just by failing to throw that circuit breaker, but also by imagining I could be more than Rose Tico, maintenance tech.

But that wasn't fair. I did my best. And that's what makes someone a hero, right? Not whether you succeed or fail, but whether you're brave enough to risk everything trying.

I've done that—as a flight engineer on a Resistance bomber, and in Canto Bight, and aboard Snoke's ship, and flying a ski speeder. And I've got so many reasons to keep trying. I've got the memories of my sister, and my family and homeworld. And I always will have those. But I've also got my fellow Resistance fighters. And I've got Finn.

IT'S LIKE I TOLD HIM ON CRAIT: WE'LL WIN BY SAVING WHAT WE LOVE. MY FIGHT IS FAR FROM OVER, AND NOW I KNOW WHAT I'M FIGHTING FOR.

Studio Fun International
An imprint of Printers Row Publishing Group
A division of Readerlink Distribution Services, LLC
10350 Barnes Canyon Road, Suite 100, San Diego, CA 92121
www.studiofun.com
© & TM 2018 Lucasfilm, Ltd.
Written by Jason Fry
Illustrated by Cyril Nouvel and Sam Gilbey
Designed by Tiffany Meador-LaFleur
Cover designed by Mariel Lopez-Cotero

All rights reserved. No part of this publication may be reproduced, distributed, or transmitted in any form or by any means, including photocopying, recording, or other electronic or mechanical methods, without the prior written permission of the publisher, except in the case of brief quotations embodied in critical reviews and certain other noncommercial uses permitted by copyright law.

Studio Fun International is a registered trademark of Readerlink Distribution Services, LLC.

All notations of errors or omissions should be addressed to Studio Fun International, Editorial Department, at the above address.

ISBN: 978-0-7944-4105-0

Manufactured, printed, and assembled in Stevens Point, WI, United States of America.

First printing, February 2018. WOR/02/18

22 21 20 19 18 1 2 3 4 5

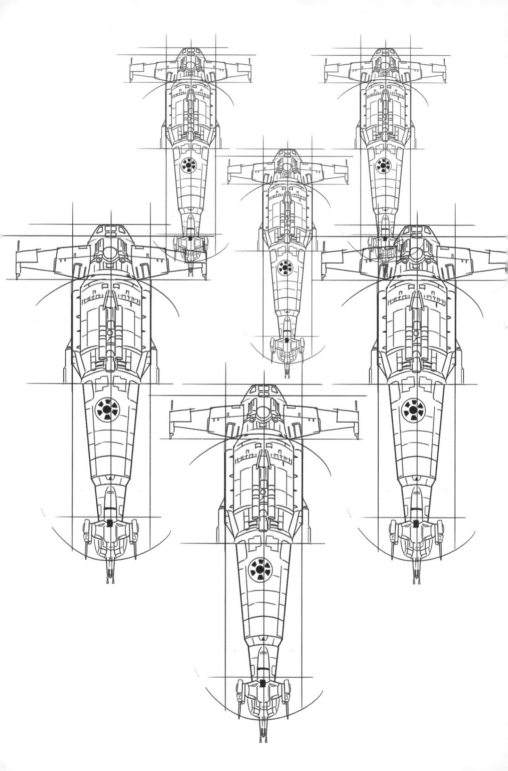